STAR WARS

EPISODE IV
A NEW HOPE

STORY AND SCREENPLAY BY
GEORGE LUCAS

TOKYOPOP®

HAMBURG • LONDON • LOS ANGELES • TOKYO

Editor - Rob Tokar
Contributing Editor - Robert Langhorn
Graphic Designer and Letterer - Anna Kernbaum
Cover Designer - Raymond Makowski
Graphic Artist - Louis Csontos

Digital Imaging Manager - Chris Buford
Pre-Press Manager - Antonio DePietro
Production Managers - Jennifer Miller and Mutsumi Miyazaki
Senior Designer - Anna Kernbaum
Art Director - Matt Alford
Senior Editor - Elizabeth Hurchalla
Managing Editor - Jill Freshney
VP of Production - Ron Klamert
Editor-in-Chief - Mike Kiley
President & C.O.O. - John Parker
Publisher & C.E.O. - Stuart Levy

E-mail: info@tokyopop.com
Come visit us online at www.TOKYOPOP.com

A **TOKYOPOP** Cine-Manga® Book
TOKYOPOP Inc.
5900 Wilshire Blvd., Suite 2000
Los Angeles, CA 90036

Star Wars: A New Hope

Special thanks to Paul Southern, Amy Gary,
Sue Rostoni and Valentina Dose.

ISBN: 1-59532-895-5

First TOKYOPOP® printing: May 2005

10 9 8 7 6 5 4 3 2 1

Printed in China

LUKE SKYWALKER:
FARM BOY FROM
TATOOINE

DARTH VADER:
LORD OF THE SITH

CHEWBACCA:
WOOKIEE AND
HAN SOLO'S PARTNER

HAN SOLO:
SMUGGLER

SEE-THREEPIO (C-3PO):
PROTOCOL DROID

LEIA ORGANA:
PRINCESS, SENATOR
AND REBEL LEADER

ARTOO-DETOO (R2-D2):
ASTROMECH DROID
AND SEE-THREEPIO'S
SIDEKICK

OBI-WAN KENOBI:
JEDI MASTER

3

A long time ago in a galaxy far, far away....

It is a period of civil war. Rebel spaceships, striking from a hidden base, have won their first victory against the evil Galactic Empire.

During the battle, Rebel spies managed to steal secret plans to the Empire's ultimate weapon, the *Death Star*, an armored space station with enough power to destroy an entire planet.

Pursued by the Empire's sinister agents, Princess Leia races home aboard her starship, custodian of the stolen plans that can save her people and restore freedom to the galaxy....

AS A HUGE EXPLOSION ROCKS THE SMALL SHIP, DROIDS C-3PO AND R2-D2 STRUGGLE TO KEEP THEIR FOOTING.

OH MY! WE'RE DOOMED! THERE'LL BE NO ESCAPE FOR THE PRINCESS THIS TIME!

THE IMPERIAL STAR DESTROYER'S TRACTOR BEAM SLOWLY PULLS THE VESSEL INTO ITS DOCK...

...AND THE REBEL SOLDIERS PREPARE FOR BOARDING BY IMPERIAL TROOPS.

AS IMPERIAL STORMTROOPERS ENTER THE SHIP, A FIERCE BATTLE ENSUES.

WITH THE REBELS IN RETREAT, DARTH VADER, LORD OF THE SITH, BOARDS THE SHIP.

THE STORMTROOPERS BEGIN THEIR SEARCH.

There's one! Set for stun!

She'll be all right. Inform Lord Vader we have a prisoner!

Darth Vader! Only you could be so bold! The Imperial--

Don't play games with me, Your Highness! You weren't on any mercy mission this time! You are part of the Rebel Alliance and a traitor! Take her away!!

Lord Vader, the battle station plans are not aboard this ship! An escape pod was jettisoned during the fighting, but no life forms were aboard.

She must have hidden the plans in the escape pod. Send a detachment down to retrieve them, Commander. There'll be no one to stop us this time!

IN THE GARAGE...
Well, my little friend, you've got something jammed in here real good...
Huh?! What's this?
Help me, Obi-Wan Kenobi. You're my only hope!
Who is she? She's beautiful!
I'M NOT SURE, SIR. ARTOO CLAIMS TO BE THE PROPERTY OF AN OBI-WAN KENOBI AND IT'S A PRIVATE MESSAGE FOR HIM.

That wizard's just a crazy old man. Tomorrow, I want you to get that droid's memory erased. It belongs to us now.
...I was also thinking about our agreement. And if these new droids work out, I want to transmit my application to the Academy this year!
Before the harvest?! That's when I need you the most! We'll make enough this year that I can hire some more hands and you can go to the Academy next year. I promise.
Where are you going?
It looks like I'm going nowhere. I have to finish cleaning those droids.

Luke's just not a farmer, Owen. He has too much of his father in him!

That's what I'm afraid of.

AS THE TWIN SUNS OF THE PLANET TATOOINE SET, LUKE RETURNS TO THE GARAGE AND FINDS...

?!

PLEASE DON'T DEACTIVATE ME, SIR! I TOLD HIM NOT TO GO, BUT HE KEPT BABBLING ABOUT HIS MISSION...

Oh no!

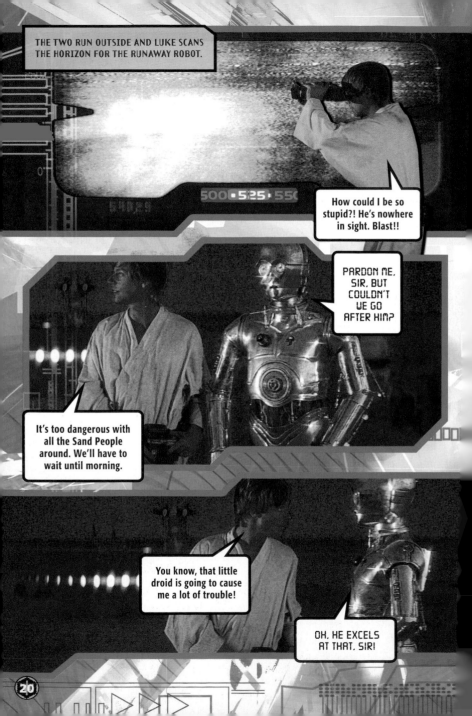

AS IF FROM NOWHERE, A SAND PERSON JUMPS IN FRONT OF LUKE, KNOCKING HIM TO THE GROUND.

URGH! URGH! URGH!

!!!

FROM HIS HIDING PLACE, R2 WATCHES AS THE SAND PEOPLE IGNORE LUKE'S UNCONSCIOUS BODY AND START TO RANSACK THE SPEEDER.

SUDDENLY, THE CANYON IS FILLED WITH A HIGH-PITCHED WAIL AS A FIGURE APPROACHES. STARTLED, THE RAIDERS QUICKLY FLEE THE SCENE.

STILL IN HIS HIDING PLACE. R2 WATCHES AS THE FIGURE APPROACHES AND KNEELS IN FRONT OF LUKE.

?!

SLOWLY, LUKE COMES AROUND.

Come here, my little friend. Don't be afraid, he'll be all right!

Ben...Ben Kenobi? Boy, am I glad to see you!

The Jundland Wastes are not to be traveled lightly. Tell me, young Luke, what brings you out this far?

This little droid...

THE GROUP MAKES ITS WAY TO OBI-WAN KENOBI'S HOME.

You fought in the Clone Wars?

Yes. I was once a Jedi Knight, the same as your father.

Which reminds me, I have something here for you.

Your father wanted you to have this when you were old enough, but your uncle wouldn't allow it. He feared you'd follow old Obi-Wan on some damned-fool idealistic crusade like your father did!

What is it?

Your father's lightsaber. This is the weapon of a Jedi Knight. Not as clumsy or random as a blaster. A more civilized weapon for a more civilized age…

How did my father die?

A young Jedi named Darth Vader, who was a pupil of mine until he turned to evil, helped the Empire hunt down and destroy the Jedi Knights.

He betrayed and murdered your father. Vader was seduced by the dark side of the Force.

The Force?

The Force is what gives a Jedi his power. It's an energy field created by all living things. It surrounds us and penetrates us. It binds the galaxy together.

AS LUKE RESUMES REPAIRS ON C-3PO...

Oh, I saw part of a message...

I seem to have found it.

28

General Kenobi, my ship has fallen under attack. I have placed information vital to the survival of the Rebellion into the memory systems of this R2 unit. You must see it delivered safely to Alderaan. Help me, Obi-Wan Kenobi, you're my only hope!

OBI-WAN THINKS QUIETLY FOR A MOMENT, THEN TURNS TO LUKE.

You must learn the ways of the Force if you are to come with me to Alderaan!

I'm not going to Alderaan! I can take you as far as Anchorhead. You can get a transport there to Mos Eisley or wherever you're going.

You must do what you feel is right, of course.

MEANWHILE, PRINCESS LEIA IS BEING HELD CAPTIVE ABOARD THE DEATH STAR, THE EMPIRE'S DEADLIEST BATTLE STATION.

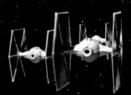

And now, Your Highness, we will discuss the location of your hidden Rebel base.

AS A MIND PROBE FLOATS MENACINGLY TOWARD THE PRINCESS...

!!

...THE CELL DOOR SLIDES SHUT, MASKING THE SCREAMS WITHIN, AND A LONE IMPERIAL OFFICER RETURNS TO HIS POST.

BACK ON TATOOINE, OBI-WAN AND LUKE DISCOVER THE BATTLE-SCARRED REMAINS OF THE JAWAS' SANDCRAWLER.

Why would Imperial troops want to slaughter Jawas? Unless…

…unless they traced the robots here and learned who the Jawas sold them to. And that would lead them to the farm!

Wait, Luke! It's too dangerous!

LUKE RETURNS TO OBI-WAN AND THE DROIDS TO TELL THEM THE NEWS.

There's nothing you could have done, Luke. If you had been there, you'd have been killed too, and the droids would now be in the hands of the Empire.

SOON, THE GROUP MAKES ITS WAY TO MOS EISLEY SPACEPORT TO FIND PASSAGE TO ALDERAAN.

I want to come with you to Alderaan. There's nothing for me here now. I want to learn the ways of the Force and become a Jedi like my father!

33

THEY PULL UP IN FRONT OF A RUN-DOWN CANTINA ON THE OUTSKIRTS OF THE SPACEPORT...

Do you really think we're going to find a pilot here that'll take us to Alderaan?

Most of the best freighter pilots can be found here. Only watch your step. This place can be a little rough!

This is Chewbacca. He's first mate on a ship that might suit our needs!

CHEWBACCA LEADS THEM TO A BOOTH...

Han Solo. I'm captain of the Millennium Falcon. Chewie here tells me you're looking for passage to the Alderaan system.

Yes, indeed. If it's a fast ship.

Fast ship? I've made the Kessel Run in less than 12 parsecs! She's fast enough for you, old man! What's the cargo?

Only passengers. Myself, the boy, two droids and no Imperial entanglements.

Well, that's the real trick, isn't it? And it's going to cost you something extra. Ten thousand, all in advance!

We can afford to pay you two thousand now, plus fifteen when we reach Alderaan.

Seventeen, huh? Okay. You guys have got yourself a ship. We'll leave as soon as you're ready. Docking bay ninety-four.

AFTER LUKE AND OBI-WAN LEAVE...

Seventeen thousand! These guys must really be desperate! This could really save my neck! Get back to the ship and get her ready!

You'll have to sell your speeder.

That's okay. I'm never coming back to this planet again!

38

ON THE DEATH STAR, DARTH VADER REPORTS TO GOVERNOR TARKIN ON THE INTERROGATION OF THE PRINCESS.

Her resistance to the mind probe is considerable.

Perhaps she'll respond to an alternative form of persuasion. Commander, set your course for Princess Leia's home planet of Alderaan!

RETURNING TO DOCKING BAY 94, HAN HAS SOME UNEXPECTED VISITORS.

Jabba!

<Han, why did you fry poor Greedo like that? Where would I be if every pilot who smuggled for me dumped their shipment at the first sight of an Imperial starship? It's not good for business.>

If you've got something to say to me, come see me yourself!

I've got a charter now and I can pay you back, plus a little extra. I just need some more time.

<Han, my boy, if you disappoint me again, I'll put a price on your head so large you won't be able to go near a civilized system for the rest of your short life.>

41

MEANWHILE, LUKE AND OBI-WAN MAKE THEIR WAY TO THE HANGAR, UNAWARE THAT THEY ARE BEING FOLLOWED BY AN IMPERIAL SPY...

What a piece of junk!!

She'll make point-five past light speed. She may not look like much, but she's got it where it counts, kid! We're a little rushed, so if you'll get on board, we'll get out of here!

OUTSIDE THE HANGAR, THE SPY ALERTS A SQUAD OF STORMTROOPERS TO THE GROUP'S WHEREABOUTS.

Stop that ship! Blast them!

HAN RUSHES ON BOARD THE MILLENNIUM FALCON WHILE REPELLING THE ATTACK.

AAAAAGH!!!

MEANWHILE, ON THE DEATH STAR...

Governor Tarkin! I recognized your foul stench when I was brought on board!

Charming to the last. Princess Leia, since you are reluctant to tell us the location of the Rebel base, I have decided to test this station's destructive power on your home planet of Alderaan!

No! Alderaan is peaceful. We have no weapons! You can't possibly...

You prefer another target? A military target? I grow tired of asking this. Where is the Rebel base?!

Dantooine.
They're on
Dantooine.

You see, she can be reasonable.
Continue with the operation.
You may fire when ready.

What?!

You're far too trusting.
Dantooine is too remote
to make an effective
demonstration. But don't
worry, we will deal with your
Rebel friends soon enough!

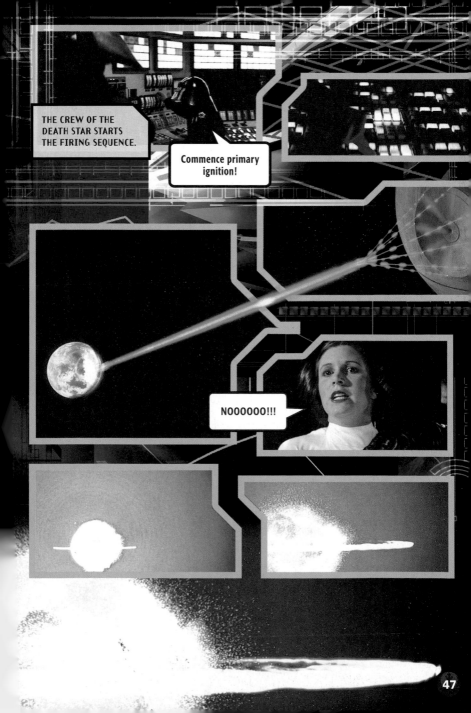

MEANWHILE, AS OBI-WAN TEACHES LUKE HOW TO USE THE FORCE...

Are you all right? What's wrong?

I felt a great disturbance in the Force...as if millions of voices suddenly cried out in terror and were suddenly silenced. I fear something terrible has happened!

BACK ON THE DEATH STAR...

Our scout ships have reached Dantooine. They found the remains of a Rebel base, but they estimate that it has been deserted for some time.

She lied to us! Terminate her...immediately!

AS THE MILLENNIUM FALCON NEARS ITS DESTINATION, HAN BRINGS THE SHIP OUT OF HYPERSPACE WITH UNEXPECTED RESULTS...

What's going on?

We've come out of hyperspace into a meteor shower. Our position is correct, except... no Alderaan!

What?! Where is it?

Destroyed! By the Empire!

That's impossible! It'd take a thousand ships with more firepower than I...

SUDDENLY, A LONE IMPERIAL TIE FIGHTER RACES PAST THE SMUGGLER'S SHIP.

AS THE MILLENNIUM FALCON IS PULLED IN, IT IS DWARFED BY THE BATTLE STATION.

Clear bay 2037! We are opening the magnetic field!

We've captured a freighter entering the remains of the Alderaan system. Its markings match those of a ship that blasted its way out of Mos Eisley.

They must be trying to return the stolen plans to the Princess. She may yet be of some use to us.

SOON...

51

IN THE DOCKING BAY CONTROL ROOM, AN OFFICER TRIES TO CONTACT THE SOLDIERS GUARDING THE FALCON.

TK-421. Why aren't you at your post?

FROM THE CONTROL ROOM, THE OFFICER SEES THE TROOPER EMERGING FROM THE SHIP AND TAPPING HIS HELMET TO INDICATE A FAULTY TRANSMITTER.

ON HIS WAY TO CHECK OUT THE PROBLEM, THE OFFICER IS CONFRONTED BY SOMETHING TOTALLY UNEXPECTED...

RUUUUHRR!!

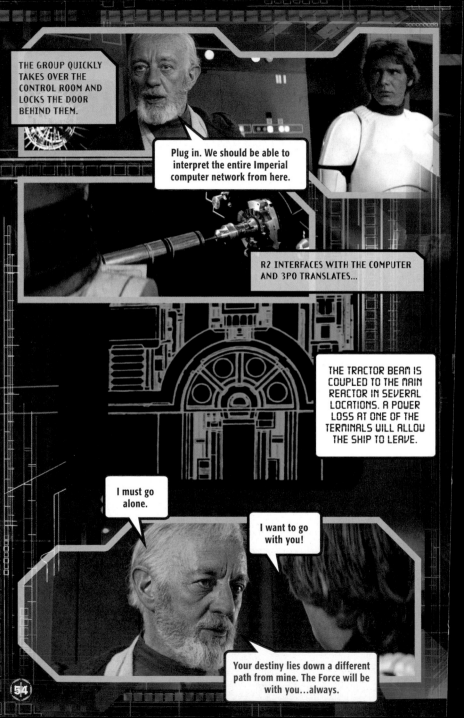

WITH LUKE AND HAN JOINING THE FRAY, ALL HELL BREAKS LOOSE IN THE DETENTION BLOCK.

WITH THE DETENTION BLOCK UNDER THEIR CONTROL, HAN CHECKS TO SEE WHICH CELL THE PRINCESS IS IN.

Here it is...cell 2187. You go get her!

THE PRINCESS GRABS LUKE'S WEAPON AND BLASTS A HOLE IN A NEARBY HATCH.

What the hell are you doing?!

Into the garbage chute, flyboy!

ONE BY ONE, THEY ALL LEAP IN...

YAHOOO!!

LUKE!!!

THERE IS A LOUD METALLIC CLANGING NOISE AND LUKE RESURFACES.

What happened?

I don't know, it just let go of me and disappeared!

I've got a very bad feeling about this...

SUDDENLY, THE WALLS OF THE CHAMBER START TO MOVE IN...

Don't just stand there! Try and brace it with something!

MEANWHILE, THE DROIDS HAVE RETURNED TO THE DOCKING BAY. USING A COMLINK FROM THE CONTROL ROOM, 3PO CONTACTS LUKE.

ARE YOU THERE, SIR?

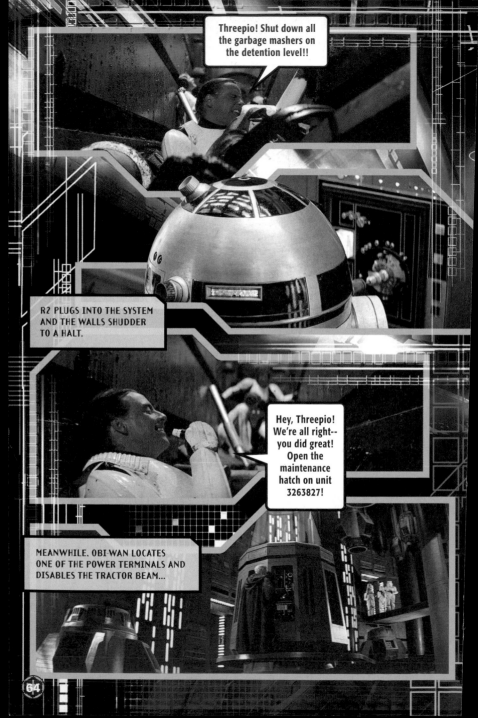

SUDDENLY, FROM ONE LEVEL UP ON THE OTHER SIDE OF THE CHASM, A STORMTROOPER STARTS FIRING AT THEM.

THINKING QUICKLY, LUKE USES THE GRAPPLING HOOK FROM HIS UTILITY BELT...

...TO SWING HIMSELF AND LEIA TO SAFETY.

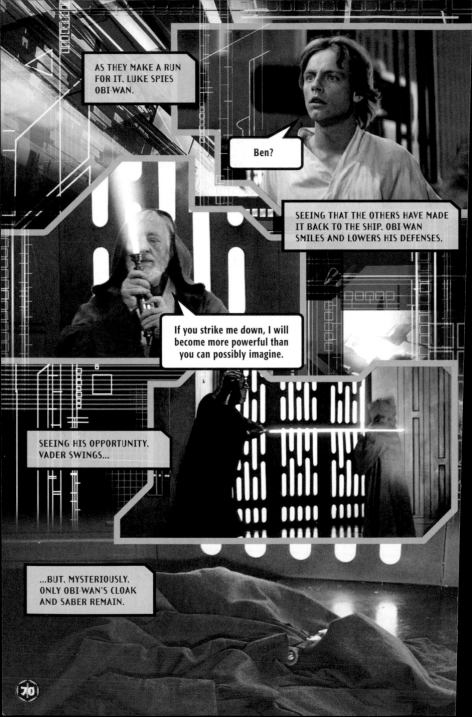

NOOOO!!!

ALERTED, THE TROOPS TURN AND FIRE.

SUDDENLY, LUKE HEARS OBI-WAN'S VOICE.

Run, Luke! Run!

LUKE HEEDS THE JEDI MASTER AND BOLTS FOR THE SHIP.

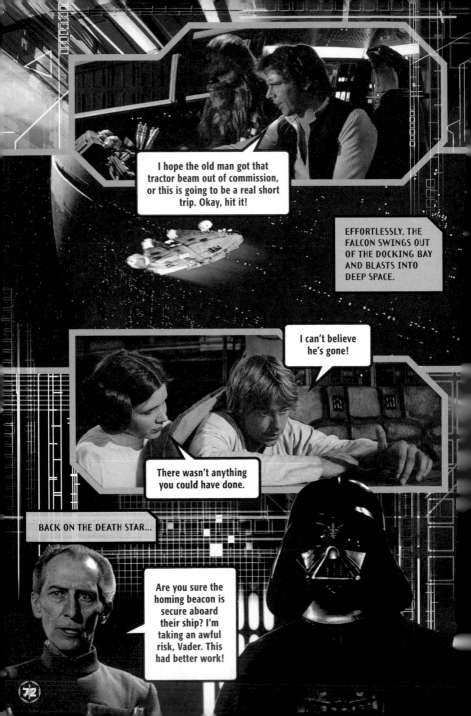

SOON, THE MILLENNIUM FALCON LANDS AT THE REBEL BASE ON THE FOURTH MOON OF THE PLANET YAVIN.

You're safe! When we heard about Alderaan, we feared the worst!

We have no time for our sorrows, Commander. You must use the information in this R2 unit to plan the attack. It's our only hope!

AS THE REBELS RUSH TO ANALYZE THE INFORMATION STORED IN R2, THE DEATH STAR OMINOUSLY APPROACHES YAVIN 4.

The battle station's defenses are designed around a large-scale assault. A small one-man fighter should be able to penetrate the outer defense, but it won't be easy. You have to maneuver down this trench to this point.

The target is only two meters wide. It's a small thermal exhaust port which leads directly to the main reactor. The shaft is ray-shielded, so you'll have to use proton torpedoes.

That's impossible, even for a computer!

It's not impossible. I used to bull's-eye womp rats in my T-16 back home. They're not much bigger than two meters!

Then man your ships! And may the Force be with you!

74

ON THE WAY TO HIS SHIP, LUKE FINDS HAN LOADING CARGO ONTO THE FALCON...

So...you got your reward and you're just leaving?

That's right, yeah! What good's a reward if you ain't around to use it? Besides, attacking that battle station ain't my idea of courage. It's more like suicide!

Well, take care of yourself, Han. I guess that's what you're best at, isn't it?

Hey, Luke...

...may the Force be with you!

THE HANGAR BUZZES WITH ACTIVITY AS PILOTS AND CREWMEN MAKE LAST-MINUTE PREPARATIONS.

WITH A DEAFENING ROAR, THE FIGHTERS TAKE OFF FOR BATTLE.

Standby alert! The Death Star will be in range in fifteen minutes!

All wings report in!

Red 10 standing by!

Red 3 standing by!

Red 6 standing by!

Red 2 standing by!

Red 5 standing by!

THE REBEL PILOTS FIGHT VALIANTLY AGAINST OVERWHELMING ODDS...

...BUT THEY'RE SYSTEMATICALLY SHOT DOWN UNTIL ONLY LUKE AND HIS WINGMEN REMAIN.

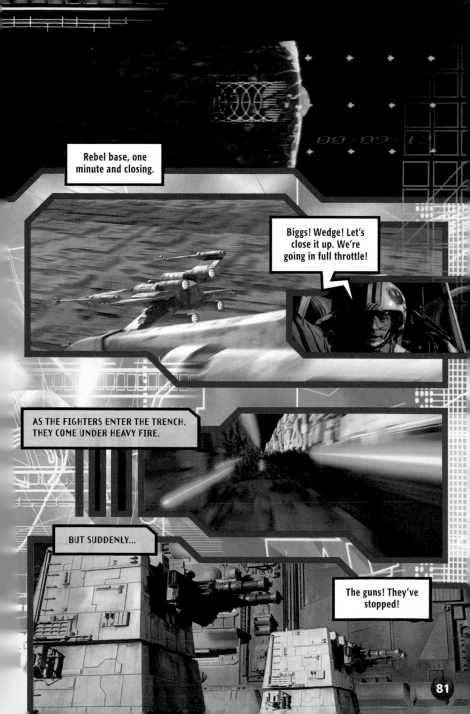

Rebel base, one minute and closing.

Biggs! Wedge! Let's close it up. We're going in full throttle!

AS THE FIGHTERS ENTER THE TRENCH, THEY COME UNDER HEAVY FIRE.

BUT SUDDENLY...

The guns! They've stopped!

AS HE APPROACHES THE END OF THE TRENCH, LUKE SWITCHES ON HIS TARGETING COMPUTER.

SUDDENLY, HE HEARS THE VOICE OF OBI-WAN...

Use the Force, Luke!

Click!

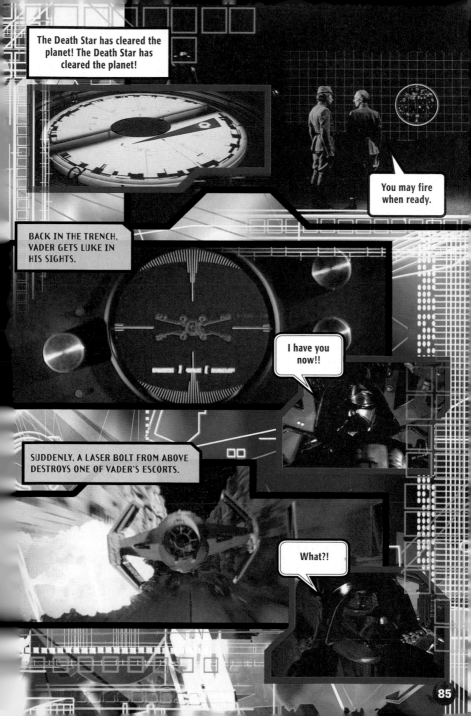

The Death Star has cleared the planet! The Death Star has cleared the planet!

You may fire when ready.

BACK IN THE TRENCH, VADER GETS LUKE IN HIS SIGHTS.

I have you now!!

SUDDENLY, A LASER BOLT FROM ABOVE DESTROYS ONE OF VADER'S ESCORTS.

What?!

USING THE FORCE, LUKE FIRES THE TORPEDOES DIRECTLY INTO THE SMALL TARGET.

AS THE REBELS RACE AWAY...

...AN UNSTOPPABLE CHAIN REACTION BUILDS WITHIN THE DEATH STAR'S CORE.

Great shot, kid! That was one in a million!

THOUGH THEIR STRUGGLE IS FAR FROM OVER...

...THE REBEL ALLIANCE GATHERS TO HONOR THE HEROES...

BLEEEEP!

...WHO FIGHT TO RESTORE FREEDOM TO THE GALAXY.

BEHIND THE SCENES

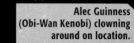

Alec Guinness (Obi-Wan Kenobi) clowning around on location.

Kenny Baker (R2-D2) breaks for lunch.

Still from the deleted scene where Biggs (Garrick Hagon) tells Luke (Mark Hamill) that he intends to join the Rebels.

David Prowse (Darth Vader) tries on an early prototype helmet.

Peter Mayhew (Chewbacca), Harrison Ford (Han Solo) and Mark Hamill (Luke Skywalker) share a humorous moment.

The REAL Landspeeder.

Track camera shooting the opening prologue.

The crew of Industrial Light & Magic shooting a miniature explosion for the Death Star battle sequence.

BEHIND THE SCENES

Peter Mayhew (Chewbacca) gets some last-minute grooming.

George Lucas compares lightsaber techniques with Alec Guinness (Obi-Wan Kenobi).

Crew members assist Anthony Daniels (C-3PO).

Kenny Baker (R2-D2), Mark Hamill (Luke Skywalker), George Lucas and Anthony Daniels (C-3PO) on location in Tunisia.

Mark Hamill (Luke Skywalker) and Carrie Fisher (Princess Leia) prepare to swing across the chasm...before the visual effects are added in.

A stormtrooper takes a nap break outside the set.

George Lucas and Greedo on the cantina set.

Creating a Star Destroyer model at Industrial Light & Magic.